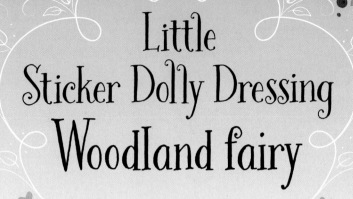

Little Sticker Dolly Dressing Woodland fairy

Written by Fiona Watt
Illustrated by Lizzie Mackay
Designed by Antonia Miller

T0381961

Contents

Willow the woodland fairy

Willow lives in a treehouse in Fairyland.
She is friends with the other fairies that live there,
and with all the little woodland creatures too.

Dress Willow in her fairy clothes, then decorate
the pages with the rest of the stickers.

Sweetpea

Magical dewdrops

As the sun slowly rises in the sky,
Sweetpea and Marigold tiptoe outside to collect
droplets of dew from glistening spiders' webs.

Marigold

Dewberry

Willow

Fairy garden

Flowers are dancing in the gentle breeze
that's swirling around Willow's garden.
The fairies are gathering flowers
to decorate their treehouses.

Serena

Dawn chorus

At the beginning of each new day, Serena and Melody love to listen to the tweets, twitters and chirps of the wild woodland birds.

Melody

Violet

Picking berries

Willow loves searching for ripe berries
that shine like rich jewels in the sunlight.
She fills her basket and takes them home
to eat with her fairy friends.

Willow

11

Gathering acorns

High in the treetops, tiny fairies are fluttering between the branches, collecting acorns for squirrels to eat during the cold winter months.

Petunia

Fairy dust

Willow and Petunia are collecting pollen
from sweet-smelling flowers. They fly from flower to
flower gathering a little from each one, that later
they will turn into magical fairy dust.

Willow

Briar

Feeding the birds

On snowy days, Briar and Morella bring baskets of food
to give to the woodland creatures. There are seeds
for the birds, fruit for the badgers and hedgehogs,
and tasty carrots for all the rabbits.

Morella

Clover

Cornflower

Fluttering fairies

On warm, sunny days, Clover and Cornflower love to soar high above Fairyland to fly and flutter with beautiful butterflies.

Willow

Avaline

20

Queen Ambrosia

Fairy Queen

Once a year, Ambrosia, Queen of Fairyland,
makes a royal visit to the woodland fairies.
They curtsey before her, then present her
with gifts of fruit and fresh flowers.

Lantern light

Every evening, the fairies take turns
to tiptoe through the woodland and make
sure everyone is safe in their treehouses.

Twinkle

Pippin

23

Lullaby

Before Willow goes to bed, she sings soothing lullabies
to the woodland creatures to send them to sleep.

First published in 2019 by Usborne Publishing Ltd., Usborne House, 83-85 Saffron Hill, London, EC1N 8RT, England. www.usborne.com
Copyright © 2019 Usborne Publishing Ltd. The name Usborne and the devices 🎈🪂 are Trade Marks of Usborne Publishing Ltd. All rights reserved. No part of this publication may be reproduced, stored in a retrieval system, or transmitted in any form or by any means, electronic, mechanical, photocopying, recording or otherwise without the prior permission of the publisher. First published in America 2019. UE